DESERT NIGHT

by James Swinney
illustrated by Sarah Snow

Harcourt

Orlando   Boston   Dallas   Chicago   San Diego

Visit *The Learning Site!*

www.harcourtschool.com

"Look, we are almost there," said Aunt Doli.
Lela looked up from her book and out the window
of the bus. She saw different types of cactus
growing everywhere. The earth was flat and brown.
The sky was very blue and very large.

"Those are saguaro cacti," said Aunt Doli. Lela
had read about saguaro cacti in school.

"I know about them," Lela said. "They take a
very long time to grow. They live for a very long
time," she told Aunt Doli.

"Very good, Lela," Aunt Doli said. Aunt Doli
smiled. "You're ready for the desert!"

Aunt Doli was a photographer. She took pictures of wild animals. Magazines and book companies paid her for her pictures.

Aunt Doli traveled all over the world. She had gone to the Arctic. She had taken pictures of polar bears, walruses, and whales. She had taken pictures of penguins in Antarctica.

Now she was going to photograph the animals of the American desert. She asked Lela to come along. Lela had never been to the desert. She was very excited!

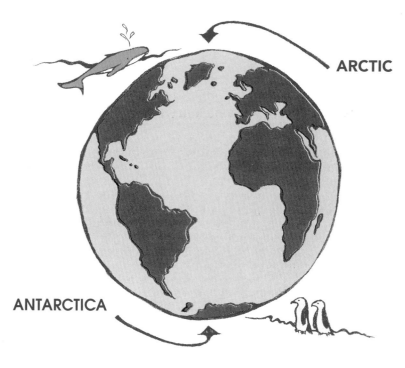

ARCTIC

ANTARCTICA

Lela and her aunt were going to visit Uncle Gil. Uncle Gil was Aunt Doli's brother. His house was in the desert. Uncle Gil studied animal life in the desert.

Uncle Gil met them at the bus station. It was easy to recognize him. Uncle Gil had a snake around his shoulders. The snake was black and red, and very big.

"Hey, Gil!" called Aunt Doli. "Help me with all this stuff." Lela watched Uncle Gil carefully. "Ugh! Is he coming over with that snake?" Lela thought to herself.

"Let's get our bags, Lela," Aunt Doli said. Lela snapped out of her daze.

Lela followed Aunt Doli and Uncle Gil to the car. Uncle Gil had cages in the back of his car. He opened a cage and placed the snake in it.

"Don't worry about Stan," Uncle Gil said. He smiled at Lela. "Stan is a king snake. King snakes are not poisonous. They are harmless to people."

Stan coiled up in a corner of the cage. Lela got in the car and sat in the back seat. "I hope Stan stays in his cage," Lela thought. She kept her face in her book the whole way to the house.

Uncle Gil showed Lela around his house. His workroom was amazing. On a worktable was a

microscope. There were cages and tanks everywhere. Some of the cages had snakes. Some had lizards.

"Uncle Gil is a scientist," Aunt Doli explained to Lela. "He studies reptiles such as snakes, lizards, and alligators. Uncle Gil is an expert on snakes."

"There are many snakes in the desert, Lela. Some are poisonous and are harmful," Uncle Gil said.

"Are these snakes harmful?" Lela asked.

"No. The snakes in this room are harmless to people. They won't hurt you," Uncle Gil said. Something on a bookshelf caught Lela's eye.

It was the most beautiful rock she had ever seen. "Oh, Uncle Gil, what is this?"

"That's called a geode," said Uncle Gil. "A geode is a hollow rock with crystals inside."

The crystals were purple. "Oh, these are beautiful," sighed Lela. "Can I pick this geode up?"

"Sure," responded her uncle. "I found it in the desert."

Lela started to pick it up. Then she pulled back her hand quickly. Next to the geode was something very long. Lela could almost see

through it. It looked like a snake!

"That is a rattlesnake skin," explained Uncle Gil. "I found this skin near this house. As snakes grow, they shed their skins. If you see a rattlesnake, do not move quickly. The snake will go away.

"Rattlesnakes are harmful to people," warned Uncle Gil. "Their bites are poisonous. They really don't want to bite people. They use their poison to kill animals for food," he said.

Lela hoped she wouldn't see a rattlesnake in the desert.

Lela's bed had a beautiful Indian blanket on it. It was black and red. A small cactus grew in a dish on the window. "This looks like a great room," Lela thought. "But what is in that tank?"

Lela walked slowly to a large tank on the desk. Inside the tank was a very large, very furry spider.

"Yikes!" Lela yelled.

"That's a tarantula, Lela," said Uncle Gil. "These huge spiders live in some deserts. Her name is Rose. Don't worry. She is in a tank." Uncle Gil smiled at Lela.

"How can I share a room with a tarantula?" Lela thought. She didn't smile back. After dinner, Aunt Doli set up her camera in the desert. She

wanted to photograph some of the nighttime animals.

"We will see lots of bats flying overhead," she said. "I want to get some photos of the leaf-nosed bat."

"I learned in school that bats eat mostly insects," said Lela.

"That's true," said Aunt Doli. "Bats are helpful animals."

"Bats are awake at night. They sleep during the day," Lela said. As the sun was setting, they heard a howling sound.

"Do you hear that?" asked Uncle Gil. "That is a coyote. Never go near a coyote or feed one. They look like cute dogs, but they are wild."

"No problem," said Lela. "I do not want to pet a coyote. No way!"

"Look up there!" Aunt Doli pointed to the sky.

"Night birds," Lela thought. They flapped

their wings. They flew high and low. "Think again," Lela thought. "Bats! They're bats!"

Aunt Doli was busy with her camera. The camera had a long zoom lens. The camera clicked and whirred. Sometimes she would say, "Got it!" or "A little closer!" or "Turn this way!" She was talking to the bats.

It began to get very dark. Soon the sky was filled with stars. Lela looked up and tried to count them, but there were just too many!

Aunt Doli put her camera away. Uncle Gil led the way home with his flashlight. Once at home, Lela walked over to the driveway at the side of the house. She had left her book in the car.

All of a sudden she heard a rattling noise. Where was it coming from? It was so dark. Lela could not see.

Lela was afraid to move. She remembered what her uncle had said about rattlesnakes. They were harmful to humans. They were poisonous!

She stood very still. She heard the noise again: rattle, rattle, rattle. Lela tried to see the snake. She was scared. Her heart pounded.

Lela called to her aunt. "Aunt Doli," she said softly. "There's a rattlesnake!"

"Don't move!" Aunt Doli said quietly. She ran into the house. Then Uncle Gil came out. He had a long stick with a big hook on the end and a flashlight. He also had a large cage.

"Don't move, Lela!" he said. Uncle Gil pointed

the light at the rattling sound. "It's okay, Lela," he said with relief. "It's not a rattlesnake. It's a gopher snake. It is harmless to people. Its hiss sounds just like a rattlesnake. This is how that snake protects itself. It pretends to be a rattlesnake!" Uncle Gil said. "You must have scared that gopher snake!"

"I scared the snake?" Lela asked. "Well, it scared me too!"

Aunt Doli, Uncle Gil, and Lela went inside. It was time to go to sleep. Aunt Doli tucked Lela into her bed.

"So, do you like the desert?" Aunt Doli asked. She wrapped the beautiful blanket around Lela.

"Yes!" Lela said. "The desert is so different. I saw a rattlesnake skin and a geode. I heard a coyote. I saw two interesting snakes. There's a tarantula in my room. There are bats flying all around outside. There are more stars in the desert sky than I have ever seen. The desert is pretty exciting!"